SCOOBY-DOO!

MINI MYSTERIES

THE CAPTAIN'S CURSE

by John Sazaklis   Illustrated by Christian Cornia

PICTURE WINDOW BOOKS
a capstone imprint

Published by Picture Window Books, an imprint of Capstone.
1710 Roe Crest Drive
North Mankato, Minnesota 56003
capstonepub.com

Library of Congress Cataloging-in-Publication Data
Names: Sazaklis, John, author. | Cornia, Christian, 1975- illustrator.
Title: The captain's curse / by John Sazaklis ;
illustrated by Christian Cornia.
Description: North Mankato, Minnesota : Picture Window Books,
[2021] | Series: Scooby-Doo! mini mysteries
Audience: Ages 5–7 | Audience: Grades K–1
Summary: "Rocky Point Beach has seen many shipwrecks caused by
the curse of Captain Cutler's ghost. The Mystery Inc. gang puts their
day of fun in the sun on hold and dives in to investigate. Scooby-
Doo and friends are ready to wade through rough waters to solve
the mystery in this early chapter book"— Provided by publisher.
Identifiers: LCCN 2021002883 (print) | LCCN 2021002884 (ebook) |
ISBN 9781663909985 (hardcover) | ISBN 9781663921277 (paperback) |
ISBN 9781663909954 (ebook pdf)
Subjects: CYAC: Mystery and detective stories. | Shipwrecks—
Fiction. | Ghosts—Fiction. | Great Dane—Fiction. | Dogs—Fiction.
Classification: LCC PZ7.S27587 Cas 2021 (print) |
LCC PZ7.S27587 (ebook) | DDC [E]—dc23
LC record available at https://lccn.loc.gov/2021002883
LC ebook record available at https://lccn.loc.gov/2021002884

Design Element: Shutterstock/Aleksandar Karanov,
cover and back cover background

Designer: Tracy Davies

Printed and bound in the USA. 4270

TABLE OF CONTENTS

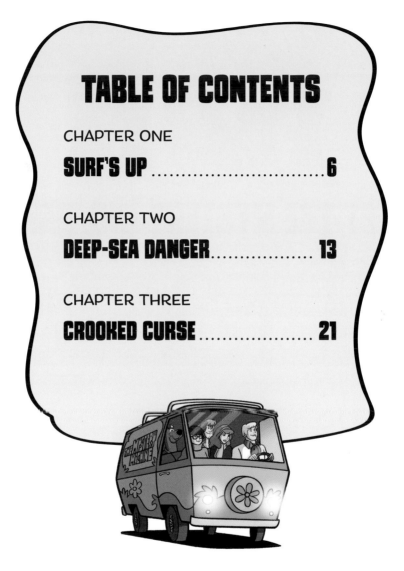

MEET THE MYSTERY INC. GANG!

SHAGGY

Norville "Shaggy" Rogers is a laid-back dude who would rather search for food than clues . . . but he usually finds both!

SCOOBY-DOO

A happy hound with a super snout, Scooby-Doo is the mascot of Mystery Inc. He'll do anything for a Scooby Snack!

FRED

Fred Jones, Jr. is the oldest member of the group. Friendly and fun-loving, he's a good sport—and good at them too.

DAPHNE

Brainy and bold, the fashion-forward Daphne Blake solves mysteries with street smarts and a sense of style.

VELMA

Velma Dinkley is clever and book smart. She may be the youngest member of the team, but she's an old pro at cracking cases.

MYSTERY MACHINE

Not only is this van the gang's main way of getting around, but it is stocked with all the equipment needed for every adventure.

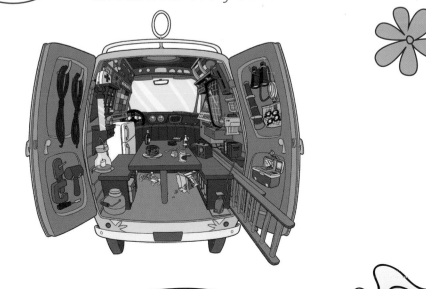

CHAPTER ONE

SURF'S UP

The Mystery Inc. gang was having fun at Rocky Point Beach. It was a day off from solving mysteries.

Daphne and Velma danced while Fred cooked. Shaggy stuffed his face. Scooby-Doo surfed.

The sun was setting while Scooby relaxed on his surfboard. Then he spotted a strange glow in the water.

"RUH-ROH!" Scooby-Doo said.

Scooby peeked underwater. He came face to face with a spooky sea diver!

"BLURG!"

Frightened out of his fur, Scooby leaped into the air. The spooky sea diver broke through the waves. He smashed the surfboard in half.

Scooby-Doo panted and paddled
all the way to his pals.

"**RELP!**" he yelped.

The four teens ran to their furry
friend. Scooby-Doo told the gang
what had happened.

"This looks like a mystery for the
members of Mystery Inc.!" Fred said.

"Like, so much for a relaxing
beach day," said Shaggy.

CHAPTER TWO

DEEP-SEA DANGER

The Mystery Inc. gang walked down the boardwalk. They found a store called Cutler's Sail Shop.

"This place sells and repairs surfboards and boats," Daphne said.

"A perfect place to start our case," said Velma.

Inside, Mystery Inc. met the owners of the shop. They told the couple what happened to Scooby's surfboard.

"We're not surprised to hear that," said Mr. Cutler.

"There are lots of accidents out in that sea," added Mrs. Cutler.

Scooby-Doo pointed to a picture of a man wearing an old diving suit.

"That is my great-grandfather, Captain Cutler," said Mr. Cutler. "He died long ago."

"The coast is cursed by the Captain's ghost!" shouted an old man. "It is a graveyard of ships."

"ZOINKS!" Shaggy yelled. "Like, did he say g-g-ghost?"

"And raveyard!" added Scooby-Doo.

"Now, Mr. Shark," said Mrs. Cutler to the old man. "That's just a silly old legend."

"We'll rent a boat and get to the bottom of this," said Fred.

"Beware the bottom of the sea!" Mr. Shark warned the teens.

It was dark when Mystery Inc. got to the dock.

"JEEPERS!" Daphne said. "Look at these glowing footprints!"

"JINKIES! They are going in opposite directions," said Velma.

"Let's split up, gang," said Fred. "Shaggy, Scooby, and I will search the sea."

"And Daphne and I will search the land," Velma said.

As the boys rowed their boat, the water began to glow. Suddenly, Captain Cutler's ghost appeared.

"ZOINKS!" screamed Shaggy.

CHAPTER THREE

CROOKED CURSE

The spooky sea diver smashed the side of the boat.

"Like, man and dog overboard!" Shaggy shouted.

Fred, Shaggy, and Scooby jumped into the water and swam for the dock.

They made it just in time. And
now the chase was on!

Fred spotted a lifesaver ring and
grabbed it.

"It's time to reel in this rascal!"
Fred said.

FLING!

Fred tossed the ring onto the diver, trapping him. Then he pulled off the ghost's helmet.

"It's Mr. Cutler!" Shaggy shouted.

Just then, Velma and Daphne arrived with Mrs. Cutler.

"And he wasn't working alone," Velma said.

"We found Mrs. Cutler controlling the pump that fed air into the diving suit," Daphne said.

"By breaking boats and surfboards on purpose, we made lots of money selling new ones," said Mr. Cutler. "And we would have made more—if not for you meddling kids!"

After the police arrested Mr. and Mrs. Cutler, the gang went back to the beach.

"Like, the only glow I want to see at night is the fire roasting my marshmallows," Shaggy said.

"SCOOBY-DOOBY-DOO!"

GLOSSARY

boardwalk—raised wooden walkway

curse—an evil spell meant to harm someone

legend—a story passed down through the years that may not be completely true

meddle—to interfere with someone else's business

pant—to breathe quickly with an open mouth

reel—pull

AUTHOR

John Sazaklis is a *New York Times* best-selling author with almost 100 children's books under his utility belt! He has also illustrated Spider-Man books, created toys for *MAD* magazine, and written for the BEN 10 animated series. John lives in New York City with his superpowered wife and daughter.

ILLUSTRATOR

Christian Cornia is a character designer, illustrator, and comic artist from Modena, Italy. He has created artwork for publishers, advertisers, and video games. He currently teaches character design at the Scuola Internazionale di Comics of Reggio Emilia. Christian works digitally but remains a secret lover of the pencil, and he doesn't go anywhere without a sketchbook in his bag.

TALK ABOUT IT

1. Would you have gone out in the boat to chase the ghost? Why or why not?

2. Do you think it was a good idea for the team to split up? Talk about your answer.

3. Were you surprised by the villains in this story? Did you think it could have been anyone else?

WRITE ABOUT IT

1. The Mystery Inc. gang uses teamwork to solve mysteries. Write about a time you used teamwork.

2. Pretend you are part of a team that solves mysteries. Make a poster about your group. Write down your team's name and members. Make a logo for your team as well.

3. Which member of the Mystery Inc. gang are you most like? Make a list of things you have in common.

Help solve mystery after mystery with Scooby-Doo and the gang!

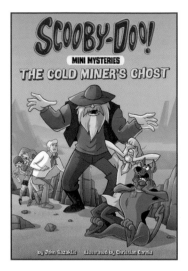

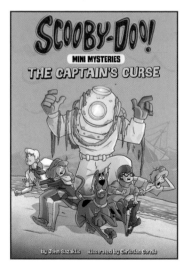